PRAISE FOR S.D. BROWN

"happily purchased for my classroom library"

LAURA, MIDDLE SCHOOL TEACHER

"Couldn't stop reading"

BONITA LOUISE RILEA

"I was hooked from the beginning."

BJ BASSETT

PRAISE FOR SCOTT PETERS

A natural and gifted storyteller

HISTORICAL NOVEL SOCIETY

"My eight year old loved this book! Couldn't put it down! In fact, he chose to read this instead of his hour of screen time!"

ANDREA, AMAZON REVIEWER

I ESCAPED THE CALIFORNIA CAMP FIRE

AMERICA'S DEADLIEST FIRE

S D BROWN

SCOTT PETERS

BDB
BEST DAY BOOKS
FOR YOUNG READERS

I Escaped The California Camp Fire (I Escaped Book Two)

Library of Congress Control Number:2019906970

ISBN: 978-1-951019-01-3 (Hardcover)

ISBN: 978-1-951019-00-6 (Paperback)

While inspired by real events, this is a work of fiction and does not claim to be historically accurate or portray factual events or relationships. References to historical events, real persons, business establishments and real places are used fictitiously and may not be factually accurate, but rather fictionalized by the author.

Photos: Paradise sign by Sharon Hahn Darlin (CC BY 2.0), Dog eating pizza by Pawsitive-Candie_N (CC BY 2.0), Puppies by Kinjen Submiter (CC by 2.0), Ambulance by Coolcaesar (CC by SA 3.0)

Cover design by Susan Wyshynski

Best Day Books For Young Readers

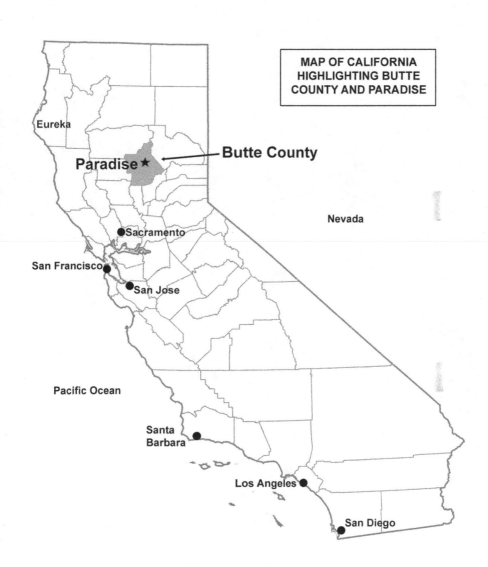

MAP OF CALIFORNIA
HIGHLIGHTING BUTTE
COUNTY AND PARADISE

Eureka

Paradise ★ ←— **Butte County**

Nevada

●Sacramento

San Francisco●
●San Jose

Pacific Ocean

Santa
Barbara ●

Los Angeles ●

San Diego ●

CHAPTER 1

THURSDAY NOVEMBER 8, 2018
PARADISE CALIFORNIA
AROUND 11:05 A.M.

FOURTEEN-YEAR-OLD TROY'S hands gripped the steering wheel so hard his knuckles hurt.

The fire had jumped the road. Explosions and flames burst on both sides, chasing the Bronco from behind—a fire-breathing monster herding them toward the forest. A forest full of nature's fuel to feed the raging blaze.

He turned to his younger sister. Her face was half-covered by a wet rag to block the smoke from entering her lungs. Above the rag, her eyes bulged in terror.

She started to scream, waving her arms and pointing. "The fire's everywhere. Look! By the road. At that house. The roof just collapsed. And look at the bakery. Flames are coming out of the windows. Turn around. Go back."

"We can't," Troy said, looking into the rearview mirror.

1

It seemed as if the entire town behind them was lit with flames.

"We have to keep going. It's our only chance."

"We're not going to make it," she said.

"Yes, we are."

He hoped the lie would morph into truth.

The fire accelerated, consuming the equivalent of a football field every second.
    — Cal Fire Official Statement

CHAPTER 2

ONE DAY EARLIER
WEDNESDAY, NOVEMBER 7, 2018
PARADISE, CALIFORNIA
AROUND 4:00 P.M.

FOURTEEN-YEAR-OLD TROY BENSON snagged the keys to the family's blue Ford Taurus from the kitchen counter. His dad had just finished drinking a glass of water and had set it in the sink. His mom scurried around like she'd be going away for a month instead of a day.

Were they ever going to leave?

Troy said, "Hey, I can load your stuff in the car and back it out of the garage for you. Okay?"

His dad grinned. "If I didn't know better, I'd think you're trying to get rid of us. Sooner than later."

Exactly, Troy thought. Once his parents left town, he'd walk to the HOLIDAY MARKET for some serious junk-food-contraband. Since his parents had opened PARADISE

HEALTH MART, he'd been drowning in organic-this and hummus-that.

He finger-shot his dad. "Wish I had a get-out-of Paradise card like you and Mom. Admit it. Living in Paradise is kind of boring."

Welcome to Paradise, California

"I'd be careful what you wish for, son," his dad said and winked. He looked at the clock on the wall. "Honey. If you still want to attend the no-host dinner, we need to get on the road."

"Almost there," Mom said. "Just one last thing."

Troy grabbed the two suitcases, lugged them into the garage and hit the remote. The garage door rumbled open like the thunder before a lightning storm. The car was parked next to his dad's SUV Bronco. The suitcases went into the car's trunk and he went into the driver's seat. Ever since he'd learned to drive the tractor on his grandparents' farm, his dad had let him pseudo-drive around the yard—mostly on the lawnmower.

At least he'd be king for twenty-four hours. His little sister would have to do what he said. Go to bed when he told her. Eat what he served. Watch what he wanted to watch on Netflix.

Using the rearview mirrors, he backed the car into the front yard and onto the yellow front lawn to make a perfect three-point turn. He grinned. At least he hadn't had to cut the grass since June because it hadn't rained in seven months. Plus, the town had water-use restrictions, which meant no outside watering.

All the yards looked the same—dried stubble, bare dirt flowerbeds, and dead bushes. Even the weeds had given up their will to live.

Everyone said the hot, dry summers were normal, but usually they'd had plenty of rain by November. This year was different. Governor Brown had declared an official end to the five-year California drought the previous April, but Paradise hadn't gotten the memo.

The only good thing about the local water-famine was that his last yard-chore had been to pull the dead plants and toss them into the compost pile in the backyard.

Troy got out of the car. It was windy and cool. After all, it was November and almost winter. Rascal, the family's large German shepherd, ran over and nudged Troy's hand. The boy rubbed her between the ears. The dog's tail slapped his leg like a drummer in a rock band.

"You're the best thing about living here," he told the dog. "Who named this place Paradise? Must have been someone's idea of a joke. Look at it. Except for the tall evergreens on the hill and around town, everything is dried up and dead. My idea of Paradise is everything green with flowers and palm trees like Hawaii. Not like this H-E-double-hockey-sticks kind of place. Minus the inferno."

There was no point in complaining. He was stuck in Paradise—a small town in Northern California along the foothills of the Sierra Nevada Mountain Range. Only 27,000 people lived in the whole town, and twenty-five percent were old—as in senior citizen old and retired.

It was an over six-hour drive to get to San Francisco and civilization.

Instead of people, Paradise had trees. Instead of streets, there was one road in and one road out. Instead of high-rise buildings, there were trailer courts tucked between small planned and unplanned neighborhoods.

If his parents had to move to the country, why hadn't they moved to the Central Valley near his grandparents? Where there was a horse to ride and a tractor to drive?

Rascal barked. The dog bounded across the yard.

She grabbed a red ball from under the skeleton of an oak tree. A black tire hung from one of the lower branches.

A gust of wind knocked the swing, making it spin. The breeze sent a few dead leaves scattering across the lawn.

Rascal ran back to Troy, dropped the ball at her master's feet, and sat.

Troy picked up the ball and tossed it high into the air. It dropped and somehow miraculously landed inside the tire. Was it the wind?

"Wow!" Troy couldn't do it again, even if he tried a million times. "Go get it, girl."

Rascal raced after the ball. She jumped on the tire, sending the black rubber Goodyear into a twirl. Rascal barked and jumped again. The branch cracked. Held for two more twists of the tire before snapping and crashing to the dry earth.

Rascal yelped.

"Come on, girl," Troy said. "It's time to go inside and hope Mom doesn't notice."

CHAPTER 3

WEDNESDAY, NOVEMBER 7, 2018
PARADISE, CALIFORNIA
AROUND 4:15 P.M.

TROY SMILED at his mom like he was listening. He wasn't. His mind was focused on his plans for the next twenty-four hours and the food he was going to eat. It was going to be stellar. Pizza. Hot dogs. Mac-N-Cheese. Chili fries. Fish sticks. Pepsi. Mountain Dew. Henry Weinhard's Root Beer. Double-stuffed Oreos. Cookie-dough ice cream. Doritos Nacho Cheese chips. And whatever else he wanted to eat. And not at the table.

"Troy, are you listening?" his mom said.

"Yeah, Mom."

"Then what did I just say?"

He held up his thumb to begin the countdown. "No friends over." Up went the index finger. "No junk food." His other fingers followed as he rattled off the rules. "Go to bed at the regular time. Get up a half hour early. Don't miss the bus." Next hand. "No fighting. No messes. Walk the dog. Feed the cat. If we have any problems, consult Mrs. Jones next door. She's a retired nurse and knows what to do in an emergency." He grinned and punched the air. "Nailed it."

"You did," his dad said. "But in case of a real emergency, call 911. Honey, we really need to get on the road."

"One last thing," Mom said.

"You said that twenty minutes ago," Dad said.

"Troy and Emma," his mom said, doing her version of Vanna White and sweeping her hand across the spotless kitchen, "this should look exactly as it does when we return." She pulled out her phone. "And so there's no argument, I'll document how things look."

She snapped shots of the big open kitchen and living area. *Click.* The sink. *Click. Click. Click.* Stove-top. Refrigerator. Microwave. *Click.* Floor. *Click. Click. Click. Click.* "Emma, use the microwave and not the stove. Remember the cookies you forgot in the oven last week? I don't want to come home to find you burned the house down. Troy, don't forget to lock up before you go to bed."

"Enough, honey," Dad said, giving Troy a wink. "If we didn't trust Troy and Emma to be responsible, we wouldn't be leaving them home alone for the night. What kind of trouble can they get into? They'll be in school all day tomorrow, and you know Mrs. Jones has an eagle-eye view from her front room window. Everything'll be fine. We'll be home tomorrow night."

"I know," Mom said. "It's just that my babies are growing up too fast."

"We're not babies," Emma chimed in. She shot Troy a look. "At least I'm not."

"That's because you're a mutant," Troy said, laughing. "A science experiment gone wrong." At his mother's frown, he added, "Just kidding. I love my little sister."

Dad pointed at the wall clock hanging over the stove, with its butter-knife hour hand and spoon minute hand.

"One last hug." Mom scooped both kids into the same tight embrace. To Troy, she said, "Be nice to your sister." To Emma, "Your brother is in charge. Do what he says."

"Do I have to?" Emma pouted.

"Come on," Dad said. "We want to get there before nightfall."

Troy grinned. His dad liked to exaggerate. It was only an hour's drive to Redding and at least three hours until sunset.

Troy and Emma waved as their parents drove around the corner and disappeared from view. Rascal barked and Midnight appeared from under a bush. Emma scooped up the kitten and cradled it like a baby.

Troy slugged his sister in the arm and yelled, "Party time!"

"Shut up, Troy." Emma pointed to Mrs. Jones' living room window with a wave and a big smile. "She's watching."

The older woman waved back from her recliner.

"Looks like her window is open. Bet she heard you."

"Don't be such a brat," Troy said and went inside with Rascal at his heels.

CHAPTER 4

THURSDAY, NOVEMBER 8, 2018
PARADISE, CALIFORNIA
AROUND 2:00 A.M.

THE CLOCK on the kitchen wall read 2:00 a.m.

Troy grinned. If his parents asked, he could truthfully say they were up extra, extra early for the school day. He'd just leave out the part that they hadn't gone to bed, yet. No foul. No penalty.

Emma would be stupid to rat him out unless she wanted to be on restriction, too.

Empty soda cans, candy wrappers, and half-eaten junk food littered the coffee table in the living room. Rascal had just wolfed down pizza crusts and was starting in on licking the empty paper plates. Midnight sniffed the carpet where Emma had spilled chili.

On TV, Kung Fu Panda had just rolled down a set of steep temple steps.

"I don't feel so good," Emma said, her hand clutching her stomach. "Maybe we should have eaten the tofu and chicken Mom left for us to reheat for dinner. Instead of this junk food."

"Not even," Troy said. "It's because we're watching this stupid movie."

He'd wanted to watch *Transformers*. At least the panda was better than Emma's favorite movie—*Mary Poppins* from the last century. "You didn't have to eat my food. You could have had the casserole."

"I'm going to tell Mom. You spent our emergency money on junk food."

"And I'll tell her you were in her makeup," Troy said, eyeing her clown lips. "Maybe you should go to bed. We can clean up in the morning before school." He grinned. "By then, Rascal and Midnight should take care of most of it."

"Okay," Emma said and picked up Midnight. "Aren't you going to bed?"

"In a little while," he said. As soon as she left the room, he shut off the lights, put on *Transformers* and turned it down low. He settled on the couch under one of his mom's crocheted blankets. Before long, sleep punched him into unconsciousness.

CHAPTER 5

THURSDAY, NOVEMBER 8, 2018
PARADISE, CALIFORNIA
AROUND 9:15 A.M.

TROY AWOKE TO DOG BREATH, a canine tongue and a cold nose nudging his face. He patted Rascal's head. "Too much pizza, girl? Can't you wait till morning?"

Rascal wined, let out a few yips and pawed his arm.

"Okay." Troy sat up on the couch and rubbed his eyes, still half asleep. "You need to go do your business. Just a minute." He reached down and felt for his shoes.

Wait. Something was off. Suddenly he was wide-awake; his eyes darted left and right. He couldn't see anything. It was black. The usual electronic lights were dead and the steady hum of the fridge silent. The electricity must be out —which was seriously *weird*. There hadn't been a storm in months.

What time was it?

Rascal began to bark, jumping on Troy. Then the dog nipped at the sleeve of his hoody and pulled.

"Okay. Okay. I'm moving." Troy stood, fumbled for his cell on the coffee table, and turned on the flashlight feature. The beam lit the room. Their food-feast remains lay strewn across the carpet like garbage art. "Wow. Look at the mess you made. Good thing Mom's not here."

The landline rang. Rascal started barking and frantically ran back and forth to the door. Whoever was calling could wait. It was the middle of the night and probably a wrong number. Plus, Troy didn't want to clean up after Rascal if she had an accident in the house. Which hadn't happened since she was a puppy.

He stumbled after Rascal and opened the door. Outside, it was pitch black. There wasn't even starlight. The wind ripped at his clothes like it was being chased by fire-breathing dragons. And smelled that way, too—smoky and warm.

Someone must have built a bonfire.

"Hurry up, girl," he said. He wanted to get back inside and back to sleep.

Rascal didn't head to her usual spot. Instead, she kept barking and barking.

"What's wrong?" he asked. She usually only got this excited when a raccoon grocery shopped in their trashcan.

"Troy?" Emma's voice shouted. Her shadow darkened the front door.

"What?"

"That was a call from my school."

Emma must be dreaming. "That's ridiculous. Your school wouldn't call in the middle of the night."

"It's not night," she said, her voice all excited and squeaky. "It's nine fifteen. In the morning."

"What?" He looked at his phone. She was right. But then why was it still dark? Were they in the middle of a solar eclipse? Mrs. Grady, his science teacher, was slipping. He looked back at his phone.

Wow. He'd missed at least fifteen text messages from his friend Jeremy. He scrolled through and read them in order. By the time he reached the last one, he knew why Rascal was acting crazy. He felt a little crazy himself.

The first one read—*where r u?*

Second one—*cutting class?*

The third to twelfth were similar jabs. Number thirteen said—*fire drill*

Fourteen—*fire for real!*

Fifteen—*yeah school's out*

The last one said—*i see flames*

CHAPTER 6

AS TROY STARED at his phone, the smoke hit him like a baseball bat. Troy's throat grew tight. His eyes burned.

Rascal barked and ran in circles.

"Shhh, girl," Troy said and patted her back. Rascal expected him to do something. His sister did, too. His parents had left him in charge—of Emma, Rascal, Midnight and the house.

"Hold on. What am I supposed to do? Sit, girl."

The dog obeyed and leaned up against Troy's leg. Her barks morphed into soft intermittent yips between low-pitched whines.

He looked up at the black sky and back to his phone.

Squinting, he reread the text messages from Jeremy. His friend liked to joke, but the dark sky, the intense wind, and the smoke weren't a game. The fire was real. Still, Jeremy could be trying to be funny. Trying to scare Troy. Or making a jealous jab, that Troy had cut class without him.

How worried should he be? He'd never been in a fire before.

His first instinct was to check the news—but no electricity meant no cable. He punched in a Google search, but it was taking forever to connect.

He finally gave up and sent a quick return text to Jeremy—*slept in R you home?*

Almost immediately, Jeremy answered—*no. on the road. u?*

Troy—*home*

Jeremy—*get out of town*

Jeremy—*NOW!!!!!!*

"Troy. I'm scared," Emma called, her dark shadow moving toward him.

"Wait there. I'm coming," he said, walking back to the house with Rascal bumping his leg at every step. "We're going to be fine. Who called?"

"My Principal. The school is sending kids home because of a fire."

"Did you ask him where it is? How close to town?"

She shook her head. "It was just his voice. A recording. I called back, but no one answered. What are we going to do?"

"First, you need to get dressed." Troy pushed her inside the house. She went.

He stood in the open doorway and stared at the dark, his mind racing. What next? Think. He was a Boy Scout, but he wasn't prepared for this situation. Still, he had to run through the options.

Okay. The best weapon against fire was water. Maybe he should hose down the house and the yard. He started to cough. The smoke seemed to be getting thicker and he put his hand to his face. How close was the fire? Was there time to soak the yard and the house enough to stop a fire? Was there even enough water?

Option two—the basement. It was made of concrete. It wouldn't burn if the fire reached their neighborhood. Maybe he, Emma, Rascal, and Midnight should wait it out there—at least until the firemen came.

He squinted in the direction of the neighbor's homes but saw only blackness. It was way too gloomy to see more than a few feet. He couldn't even make out Mrs. Jones' house, which was just next door. She had lived in Paradise forever. She should know what was going on and if they should even be worried.

But first, he'd give his dad a call.

CHAPTER 7

TROY PULLED OUT HIS CELL. Dad would tell him what to do.

Troy tapped the autodial on the screen and waited.

"Come on, come on. Answer."

When it finally answered, it went straight to voice mail. He groaned and tried his mom's phone. Hers did the same thing. He left a quick message.

"There's a fire up here. They canceled school. Call me back."

Now what?

"Hey!" he yelled at Emma's bedroom door. "I'm going next door to see Mrs. Jones."

"Wait until I'm dressed. Don't leave me here alone."

He couldn't decide if she sounded scared or was just doing her usual whine. Either way, the fire could be racing toward their house. He needed answers now. She'd have to deal with her fear. He wasn't waiting the twenty minutes it'd take for her to get ready.

"I'll be right back. Rascal's here." To the dog he ordered. "Stay, girl."

Troy hurried to the neighbor's house and knocked on the front door before opening it. "Mrs. Jones? It's Troy. Are you okay?"

"I'm in the living room. Come on in." Mrs. Jones sounded cheerful.

Troy obeyed and was greeted with the scent of cinnamon mixed with something antiseptic. It always smelled like a cross between a doctor's office and a bakery in the house. What wasn't normal was the odor of smoke in the mix.

Mrs. Jones was eighty-two and had been a nurse. She always said, *kill the germs, kill the crud.*

It must be true, Troy thought. She was never sick. "Do you know what's happening?" he asked. "Should I be worried? I tried to call my parents, but they didn't answer."

Emma burst into the room, breathless, Rascal at her side. "I told you to wait for me." She'd only gotten half dressed—flip flops, Minnie Mouse pajama top, and jeans. "You left me alone and I was scared."

"I told you I'd be right back." Troy tried to sound like his dad. Emma could be such a pain. "Stop acting like you're three. Sorry, Mrs. Jones."

"It's her first fire," Mrs. Jones said. "I understand."

"Aren't you worried?" Emma asked, the panic in her voice slowing. "It's daytime and it's dark like night. It smells like the whole town is on fire."

"Pish posh. I've lived here all my life. I've seen so many fires up here you wouldn't believe it."

"Like this?" Troy said.

"Don't worry," Mrs. Jones said. "They'll put it out. They always do."

Boom. Boom. Boom.

The three thunderous explosions blasted outside.

Rascal yipped.

"What was that?" Emma asked, her voice cracking.

CHAPTER 8

BURSTS OF FIRE glowed through Mrs. Jones' front room window. Trees looked like they were shooting into the dark sky.

"The hill's on fire," Troy said.

Another series of explosions boomed, sounding like a giant's machine gun mowing down the enemy.

Emma screamed.

Rascal flinched and quivered against Troy's leg.

More patches of fire spots erupted in the distance. Troy gulped, a sick feeling settling in his stomach.

Emma grabbed his hand.

"Don't worry, dears," Mrs. Jones said. "The firefighters will be here soon. Would you like a cinnamon roll? I baked them last night. With the electricity being on the fritz, you'll have to eat them cold but they're fresh."

"It sounds like a war is going on out there," Troy said, thinking Mrs. Jones was not taking the danger seriously. "My friend Jeremy's family left town. I think . . ." He frowned. "We should go, too."

"You young people overreact to everything." She sniffed. "It's not your fault. It's the excessive live media coverage you're exposed to. I predict this false-induced stress will cause your generation to have the highest rates of heart attacks and strokes in modern history."

"Look out the window," Troy said. Up the hill, the individual fire patches had joined into a huge bonfire. It looked like it was coming closer every second. "We have to leave. Now."

"Well, I'm not going anywhere," Mrs. Jones said. "And it would be prudent to check with your father before you make any rash decisions." She picked up her knitting needles and they began to click. "It's a long walk out of town. You'll be heading straight into the forest. That's more dangerous than staying put."

Troy didn't know what to think. She'd lived in Paradise most of her life. What she said made sense—but Jeremy's parents had decided to get their family out of town.

"I believe it's safer to stay right where we are," she said. "You wouldn't want to get in the way of the firefighters."

His dad's words came back to him. *You're in charge. Take care of your sister.*

"I told you. I've already tried to call my Dad," Troy said, "and my Mom."

"And I texted them," Emma said, talking at the same time.

"They didn't answer," Troy said.

Emma hit his arm. "That's because they're at the workshop, stupid. Remember they said we could only reach them on the hour." She rolled her eyes. "You never listen."

Troy let the snarky comment pass. At least she wasn't crying.

He checked the time. His parents wouldn't get his message or Emma's text for another twenty minutes. Did they have enough time to wait for Mom and Dad's advice?

Outside, the flames looked higher, wider, and closer. Red embers floated in the air, drifting like the tail-ends of a FOURTH OF JULY firework rocket. Only this was November eighth, two weeks before Thanksgiving.

Mrs. Jones might be right. Maybe the firefighters would put out the blaze, but where were they? Why was the fire spreading?

CHAPTER 9

TROY WISHED his dad would call. But he hadn't. It was up to Troy. He had to decide.

Stay and wait for firefighters?

Or start walking and try to get as far from the fire as possible? He pictured the one road out of town.

Through the front window, four doors down and on the opposite side of the street, a propane tank exploded into a massive firebomb. The bright fireball lit the neighborhood. Glowing debris flew as if tossed by a fire god casting destruction into the wind. Basketball-sized sparks soared into the air and then rained down onto the Merrills' and Johnsons' roofs. In seconds, their shingles began to glow.

Emma bit her lower lip, her wide eyes ping-ponging between him and the fire. Now, only the length of a football field stood between them and the advancing flames. Rascal bit Troy's sleeve and tugged.

"We're leaving," Troy said. "I think it's what Dad would tell us to do."

"Don't worry about the fire," Mrs. Jones said for like the third or fourth time. "The fire department may be taking its sweet time. But they'll come. I tell you, it's safer here than out there."

Mrs. Jones was an adult, and his parents had told him to check with her if there was a problem. Like she was semi-in-charge. So it felt wrong ignoring her advice. But it felt more wrong taking it.

They had to get out of Paradise. ASAP.

"Emma, move," Troy said and pushed his sister toward the door. "Mrs. Jones, I think you should come with us. The fire is too big and too close to stay."

"Suit yourself. See you when you get back."

Emma ran to the woman. "Don't stay, you'll die. Please, come with us. We need you to drive. Troy doesn't have a license."

"I said, I'm not leaving. This is my home. I was born here and if it's God's will, I'll die here."

"Come on, Emma," Troy shouted and grabbed her arm. "I'm sorry. We can't stay. Can't you see? The Greens' place is on fire, too. Please, Mrs. Jones. Come with us."

Mrs. Jones kept knitting.

Troy half dragged his sister from the house and ran to theirs. He led her to the front door. The hot wind pulled at their hair and clothes.

"Wait out here," he said. "I have to go through the house to get into the garage."

"Don't leave me," Emma said. "Please?"

"It's safer out here. Yell and bang on the garage door if the fire gets closer. I'll hurry. Rascal, stay."

"Where's Midnight?" Emma cried. "We can't leave Midnight behind."

"Call him, he'll come to your voice," Troy said, thinking of Jeremy's last two text messages—*get out of town NOW!!!!!!*

Why had he wasted so much time? They should have left when he read Jeremy's warning. He'd been so stupid.

"What if Midnight doesn't come?" Emma said.

"I don't have time to argue." Troy sounded as annoyed as he felt. "He will."

She started to cry. "What if he doesn't?"

Troy didn't answer. He reached for the doorknob and turned it.

CHAPTER 10

TROY TWISTED the doorknob and pulled open the front door.

Something black and furry shot from the house and he jumped.

"Midnight," Emma squeaked and bent to scoop up her baby. "Ouch. Ouch. Ouch," she said as the terrified cat climbed up her legs and tried to bury itself in her armpit. "Shhh, you're okay now. I've got you."

Troy felt relieved as he raced inside. Emma had Midnight to keep her occupied while he got the Bronco out of the garage.

The living room seemed darker and the garage pitch black. He couldn't see a thing and frantically felt for the Bronco's keys that should have been hanging on the wall. They weren't there.

Blindly he slapped the wall again, felt the row of hooks —no Bronco keys.

"No," he moaned. They had to be there.

He ran his hand down the wall and across the concrete floor—no keys. Stepping sideways, he bumped hard into a stack of plastic milk crates. They clattered onto the concrete. He slipped and stumbled over one. The hard plastic dug into his shin as he staggered to keep balance.

"Banana boogers," he muttered, like they were magic words to banish the throbbing pain in his leg. *You're not Emma. So stop panicking. And stop wasting time knocking around in the dark.*

Think.

He reached for his phone but it wasn't in his pocket. It must have fallen out when he fell.

Then he remembered. His mom kept an emergency flashlight on the kitchen counter next to the fridge. He ran back inside to get it. He flipped it on and flashed the kitchen. The beam spotlighted his backpack on the counter and the remains of what was left of last night's pig-out.

It only took a minute to grab his backpack, dump the schoolbooks, and shove crackers and a jar of Skippy peanut butter into the bag. His mom kept extra cash in the cookie jar. He snagged it just in case and shoved the money into his pocket. At the last second, Troy snatched a steak knife. They might need it. For exactly what, he didn't know.

Back in the garage, he spotted his phone. Grabbed it and flashed the light to where the keys should have been. The crazy thing is that they were hanging exactly where they always hung. Was his mind playing tricks? They weren't there three minutes ago. But they must have been.

He felt heat race to his ears. How could he be so brain-less? Maybe the smoke had clouded his judgment—at-tacking him like some video game fire-breathing monster. He needed to up his game.

He ripped the keys from the hook and hit the garage-door-opener button. When nothing happened, he felt even more stupid. Duh! Of course, the door-opener didn't work with the electricity dead.

He darted to the garage door, grabbed its metal handles and yanked. The door inched open painfully slowly, as if afraid to let the fire inside.

When he got it as high as his waist, he squatted and put the heels of both hands under it and bench-pressed the door open. It's a good thing they'd been weight lifting in PE.

Rascal and Emma stood waiting on the driveway.

"What took you so long?" Emma complained. "Did you lock up? Mom said to remember to do that when we left for school."

Great. Emma's attitude had rebounded.

"We're not going to school," he said.

Emma's PJ top was strangely lumpy. The Minnie Mouse design moved, making it look like a mutant body snatcher had invaded Emma's stomach.

"What's under your shirt?" He tried to sound patient like his dad but it wasn't easy.

"Midnight," she said. "He doesn't follow orders like Rascal. I stuffed him in my top. That way, he won't get lost."

Troy shook his head. "Not a good idea. What happens when your kitty decides to scratch his way out? Get in the Bronco. Here, take the backpack. Empty it and put Midnight in it."

He opened both doors on the passenger side of the SUV. Emma scrambled into the front seat and Rascal leaped into the back.

"I'm letting you boss me for now," Emma said and un-zipped the backpack. "But don't get used to it."

"Yes, your highness," he muttered and slammed both car doors. He spotted the case of emergency water his Mom kept in the garage. They might need it. Quickly, he threw it in the back and then hopped into the driver's seat.

"Ready?" he asked.

"Ready," she said.

He slid the key into the ignition, pumped the gas pedal, and turned the key. The engine caught briefly but then sputtered and died. Heart pounding, he tried it again. Same result.

"You said you knew how to drive," Emma said, clutching the backpack. Midnight yowled from inside. Rascal panted in the back seat.

"Shut up," he snapped.

Emma began to sniff as though trying not to cry.

"Sorry," he said. "I have to concentrate."

Hopefully, he hadn't flooded the engine. Then he'd have to wait at least ten minutes to try again. He didn't think they had time to spare. *Please? Let it start this time.* He held his breath and turned the key. The Bronco roared to life. Troy shoved the car into reverse and slammed his foot on the gas.

The SUV rocketed out of the garage and into the yard, bumping into the birdbath in the center of the lawn. He slammed on the brake and they jerked to a stop. Rascal slid off the backseat.

Emma shrieked.

"We're fine," Troy said to his sister. To the dog, he said, "Sorry, girl. Lay down."

"I think we should put our seatbelts on," Emma said. "Are you sure you know how to drive?"

"Of course I do," Troy said, clicking his seat belt. He shifted the clutch into drive and hoped his words were true. It stalled. He looked back. In the rearview mirror, all he could see was fire. Everywhere. And then it began snowing ash and embers. Flames licked the roof of their house.

He slammed to a stop and started to back up.

"What are you doing?" Emma cried.

"We can't leave Mrs. Jones. We have to make her come with us."

CHAPTER 11

STAY HERE," Troy ordered Emma and Rascal. "I'll be right back."

Head down, he jumped out onto the road. The only light came from their headlights and the sparks and flames. Suddenly the air became a blizzard, but instead of snowflakes, embers and ash pelted him and the ground.

He couldn't believe this was happening. Yesterday had been normal. Now it was crazy insane. All the houses on the block were burning.

Brushing his arms and hair, he ran to Mrs. Jones's house.

He entered without knocking. "Come on," he shouted. "You have to come with us."

"I told you. I'm not leaving," Mrs. Jones said. She sat in her chair, still knitting the baby blanket.

"Come on." He grabbed her arms, lifting her from her chair. Her knitting fell to the floor. "Look. Our house is on fire. Yours is next."

She fought him and tried to pull away. "Let go of me. I'm staying here."

"But you'll die." Troy felt sick as he released her.

She bent and picked up her knitting. "My husband died in this house. If it's my time, I'll die here, too. Then we'll be together."

The Bronco's horn made three short blasts, followed by three long blasts, followed by three more short blasts. SOS. He had to leave.

"But—"

"Just go. Your sister needs you. And remember, it was my decision to stay. Not yours."

The horn started honking again, sounding frantic.

"I'm sorry. Goodbye, Mrs. Jones." He raced back to the Bronco, jumped in, and started the car moving again.

"Where's Mrs. Jones?" Emma asked.

"She wouldn't come." His jaw felt tight.

"You should have made her," Emma said. "You would have made me."

"Yeah, I would've. You're my little sister. I'd have dragged you to the car. Or carried you. Adults are different. Kids can't tell them what to do. She wouldn't leave. Said it was her decision. Not mine."

He turned a hard right and clipped the curb with the tire. The SUV bounced down hard and Emma grabbed the dash.

"Maybe she thought it was more dangerous to ride with you than face the fire," she said.

Was Emma trying to make him feel better with her teasing? It didn't work.

He felt awful.

And frightened.

He looked back. The whole street was on fire now.

"Goodbye house," Emma whispered. "Goodbye, Mrs. Jones."

CHAPTER 12

ONE LAST TURN and they'd be on the main road heading out of town—everyone called it the Skyway to Paradise.

He rounded the corner. Got ready to punch the gas and blast out of there. Instead, he was forced to stomp on the brake and skid to a full stop.

To his horror, he realized the Skyway was jammed solid with a giant trail of bumper-to-bumper cars and trucks.

Their escape was blocked. Him and his sister, Rascal and Midnight were going nowhere. They were trapped.

And the fire was closing in.

"Put on the blinker," Emma said. "Then someone will let us in."

"Lot of good that would do," Troy snapped. "And I don't need a back seat driver telling me what to do."

He flipped the blinker on. A pickup truck gave him just enough room to join the exodus. He crept into the flow of traffic.

"See, it worked," she said. "I told you so."

Troy wished she'd shut up, but telling her that would only make her give more stupid orders. He needed to concentrate on driving. "Why don't you try to call Mom and Dad again? You said they had a break every hour on the hour. Why didn't they call?"

"Maybe they didn't get our messages," Emma said. "We have to wait until eleven to call them again. They won't pick up now." She sat silent for a whole two seconds.

"Try anyway." At least it'd give her something to do instead of arguing.

She punched the redial button. Waited. "It's Emma. I'm with Troy. Our house is on fire." She shoved the phone in her pocket and sat silent for a moment. She sniffled and wiped her cheeks. When she finally spoke, she sounded like a little girl. "Sorry I bossed you. I'm just scared."

"It's fine," he said, not bothering to make it sound like he meant it. And then added, "It looks like everyone is leaving town at the same time."

"Yeah," Emma said. "All 27,000 people."

"Minus one," Troy mumbled.

"What?"

"Minus Mrs. Jones," he said.

"It's not your fault she stayed." Emma started bouncing in her seat and pointing out the window. "Hey look! There, on the side of the road. It's Grandma Hill and her grandkids. She's waving at us."

Troy stopped in the line of traffic for the older lady. She wasn't his grandma, but everyone in town called her that. Even people older than her. Car horns behind him blared in protest. Emma rolled down her window. "Need a ride?"

Smoke rushed in like an oxygen thief. Emma began to cough.

"Bless you. Bless you," Grandma Hill said, coming up to the Bronco and gasping for breath. "My car stopped and won't start."

"Get in. Roll up the window, Emma."

Grandma Hill opened the back door. More horns started honking.

"Move over, Rascal," Troy said.

"Oh," she said, the door still wide open. "Get in, boys." Her three-year-old twin grandsons, Danny and Sammy, piled into the back seat. "I almost forgot. I left something in our car. Wait here."

Was she serious? Really? If Emma said that, he'd yell at her, but Grandma Hill was a grown up. "Hurry. Please."

The driver in the car behind them lay on the horn and didn't let up. Troy looked back and the man behind the wheel batted the air with his open palm like he could push them off the road.

"We can't stop any longer," Troy said and waved to the other driver. He shifted the Bronco into drive and they began to inch forward.

Lucky for Grandma Hill, they'd only managed to travel about ten yards before she returned lugging a cardboard box. She shoved it onto the seat. It tipped and four golden retriever puppies spilled out, yipping.

Rascal let out a few happy barks and wagged her tail. Midnight yowled from his bag.

"There's no room for the box. Get rid of it and get in," Troy said, stopping for a moment.

"Just one last trip," Grandma Hill said. "Then that's it."

The cars horns began to blare again.

"We don't have time," he said and let the car inch forward. "Please, Grandma Hill. Get in the car."

Grandma Hill ignored him. Her hand clutched the open door and she walked to keep pace. "It will only take me a minute."

"Whatever it is, you don't need it," Troy said. "Get in."

"You don't understand," she said, beginning to sound like a retired schoolteacher. "The boys need their car seats. It's against California law for them to ride in a vehicle without them. Dangerous even."

"Car seats?" Emma said. "Can't you see the flames?"

"Danger," Troy said, trying not to yell at Grandma

Hill, "is the fire on the hill. It's getting closer and we need to get out of here." *What was with these old people—first Mrs. Jones and now Grandma Hill? Couldn't they see the fire eating its way toward them?*

The traffic started to move a little faster. The speedometer inched up to ten miles an hour.

"If a cop spots them just sitting in the seat—" Grandma Hill was huffing to keep up, "he'll give you a ticket."

"Do you see any cops?" Troy asked. "Or any firefighters? We're on our own here." He slowed to five miles an hour. "Get in. Now."

"Move over, boys," Grandma Hill shouted and managed to get into the back seat and shut the door. She was gasping for breath and her words sounded almost garbled —almost, but not quite. "And you were always such a nice boy. Polite. Law-abiding."

"Law-abiding," Emma said like she was trying out a new phrase. She looked at Troy and grinned. "Troy doesn't have a license."

"Oh no," Grandma Hill said.

Troy shot Emma a look and whispered. "Don't you know when to keep your big mouth shut?"

"Pull over. I'll drive," the old lady insisted.

"It's our car," he said, thinking that if she drove like she walked, who knows where they'd end up? Probably back at her house because she left some casserole in the oven. "I'm driving."

"We'll see about that," Grandma Hill said. She pulled out her cell. "I'm reporting this to my son. He's friends with the police chief."

CHAPTER 13

EVERY CAR on the road moved southwest in a slow, steady stream—all leaving town. All in the right-hand lanes. The oncoming lanes looked strangely deserted. Troy focused on driving, his hands clenched on the steering wheel. His foot hovered between the gas pedal and the brake.

Emma hadn't said a word since he'd told her she had a big mouth. She was biting her lip and her eyes brimmed with tears.

Grandma Hill and her grandsons were in the backseat. Rascal had commandeered the rear storage space. She leaned over the backseat, tongue out, ears perked, watching the boys whisper and cuddle the puppies. Grandma Hill's lips formed a tight line.

To Troy, the almost-silence felt as oppressive as the fire.

He hadn't meant to be rude. He was scared. Maybe he should have let Grandma Hill drive—she was an adult. But he was the one responsible for his sister, Midnight and Rascal.

"Where's Mr. Hill?" he asked to break the silence.

"He went into Chico to renew his driver's license." Her lips relaxed into a sad smile. "Thank the Lord I don't have to worry about him out in this inferno."

"Do you know how it started?" Troy asked.

"Or where the firefighters are?" Emma added, giving up the silent treatment.

"I'm sure they're out fighting the fire. I bet they'll have it under control in no time. Right, boys?"

"Yeah, Grammie," they chimed in unison. One of them added, "And we're having a venture."

"An adventure, Sammy," Grandma Hill said. "We've had a lot of fires over the years and hardly anyone has ever died. You just have to stay out of the fire's way."

Troy hoped she was right.

At least he wasn't being blinded by oncoming traffic. And they were traveling a steady fifteen miles an hour.

He glanced at the fuel gauge. They had half a tank. Should be plenty to get them out of there. At least, he hoped it was.

Even though he'd traveled down Skyway a thousand times, it looked totally different this morning. On either side of the road, familiar businesses crouched like hulking, dark blobs. Ready to pounce. Or explode. The Wells Fargo Bank to the left. Dutch Brother's Coffee on the right. The CVS pharmacy.

He caught the Bronco's reflection in a window and glanced away. It all looked so unreal.

"*The wipers on the car go swish, swish, swish,*" Sammy, Danny, and Grandma Hill began to sing. "*Swish, swish, swish.*"

Emma joined in for the third, "*Swish, swish, swish. All around the town.*"

A headache began to slam dance behind Troy's eyes. It was growing hotter and smokier with every foot they traveled. Flakes of burning ash drifted across the Bronco's hood.

The sight of a packed parking lot, highlighted by the stream of headlights headed out of town, caught Troy by surprise. The lot was alive with flashlights and camping lanterns, which bobbed amongst the moving shadows of people milling around.

"Pull into the Chin Dynasty's parking lot," said Grandma Hill, coughing. "I think I see my son's truck."

The hot, dry air made it hard to see. Trying to drum up a few moist tears, he managed to squeeze off a couple blinks and squinted at where she was pointing. The lot was full. Parked cars, headlights still blazing, spilled along the dark street.

"Where? There's got to be over seventy cars. Are you sure it's your son's?" Troy asked.

"It's the only cherry red Dodge Pickup with chrome pipes. See it? Right there."

The pickup was parked next to the main road. Troy steered to the right and parked, leaving the engine running.

"There's my son," Grandma Hill said.

"Daddy, Daddy, Daddy," the twins started chanting.

"Wait here," Grandma Hill said, jumping out of the SUV. "I'll be right back."

Not again. Troy rolled down his window and called

after her. "We can't stop. We have to keep going." Quickly, he rolled it up again to keep out the smoke. Emma began to cough. The twins coughed, too.

"Dad keeps rags under the seat. Grab a bunch. Wet them down with the water bottles." He began to cough. "First tie one over your face," he said. "Then wet a couple for the boys and me."

Emma unclipped her seatbelt and set to work. When she was done, they looked like they were about to rob a bank.

To Troy's frustration, more cars streamed steadily onto the road. His fingers drummed the steering wheel. No one would ever let them back in. The traffic seemed to be moving slower while the flames spread faster down the hill.

Outside, Grandma Hill yelled, "Tom. Yoohoo. Tom."

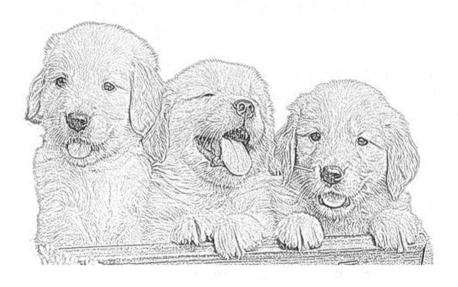

A man in blue jeans, a plaid shirt, and a baseball cap ran to meet her. Together they returned to the Bronco.

"Are these bandits my boys?" he said, lifting Sammy

and handing him to Grandma Hill. He put Danny on his shoulders and started to close the door. "Thanks for giving the family a ride."

"Don't forget the puppies," Emma said.

"Right," the man said. He set down his boy, scooped the wriggling puppies into his hands. "Come on, Danny. You're a big boy. You can walk."

"Aren't you going to leave town?" Troy asked.

"No. There's lots of pavement in this lot. It won't burn. We plan to wait it out here. Maybe you should, too. Might be safer." The man pushed the door shut with his hip.

Emma looked at Troy. "Do you think he's right? Should we stay?"

At that moment, another volley of explosions erupted. The Family Health Clinic's wall punched out from inside, sending sparks and debris onto the sidewalk. The pharmacy looked like a crematorium—all in flames. Down the block, he saw his parents' health food store. It looked okay—for the moment.

Then the front window shattered as fire danced in its aisles.

CHAPTER 14

WHAT IF HE'S RIGHT?" Emma asked a second time and stared at the packed parking lot. "Maybe we better stay here and wait it out? He's a grown-up."

"No. We need to keep going," Troy said. "Just like all these other drivers leaving town."

"But what if he's right?" she said.

"What if he's wrong?" Troy shot back. "Mrs. Jones didn't want to leave either."

He shifted into drive and tried not to picture her house in flames.

Rascal moved up between the front bucket seats, leaned over and licked Troy's neck. She barked once as if to say, *get moving.* He put on the blinker and forcefully nosed the Bronco in between a Toyota sedan and a Subaru Outback.

They drove in silence until both cell phones rang at the same time.

"Mom," Emma cried. "There's fire everywhere. And the smoke stinks."

"Dad, we're fine," Troy said, pushing up his face rag to talk. "We're in the Bronco and headed out of town."

"Who's driving?" his dad asked.

"Me."

"Why isn't Mrs. Jones driving, son?"

"She wouldn't leave." Troy felt a hitch in his voice. The car in front of him suddenly stopped. Troy slammed his foot on the brake pedal. "I . . . maybe I should hang up and save the battery. Emma can put her phone on speaker. Okay?"

"Good thinking, son."

"I'm scared, but we have Midnight and Rascal with us," Emma said and listened. "Okay. I'll put it on speaker."

"Troy," came his mom's worried voice. "Are you kids okay?"

He sucked in a deep breath. This might be the last time he ever talked to his parents. And he wanted to be strong. "Yeah. We have plenty of gas, food, and water. I hope you're not mad I'm driving without a license, but we had to leave."

"Good thinking," Dad's voice said. "You did the right thing. Where are you now?"

"We just passed Elliott Drive," Troy said. "I think. It's hard to tell. Everything's so dark. It's like midnight. All the electricity is out. There's no street lights or anything."

"Don't drive too fast," Mom said. "Take it slow and easy. Be safe."

Emma laughed. "That's funny. Troy couldn't speed if

he wanted to. There's too many cars and they're all going slow."

The cars began to move again and the Bronco inched forward.

"We love you both, so much," Mom said. Her voice sounded like she was crying. "We shouldn't have left you home alone."

"We love you, too," Emma said.

"Troy?" Dad interrupted. "Take care of your sister."

"Yes, sir."

"Emma, do what your brother tells you to do. No arguing."

"Yes, Daddy."

"Let's pray," Mom said in a quiet voice. "Dear Lord in heaven, like Shadrach, Meshach, and Abednego, give my babies safe passage through the flames, amen."

"Amen," echoed his dad and sister.

Troy wished he believed in praying and God, like the rest of his family, but he knew the Bible stuff was just a bunch of fairy tales. Because if God existed, Mrs. Jones would still be alive.

"I'm proud of you both," Dad said. "Head for Chico. We'll meet you on the road."

CHAPTER 15

THURSDAY, NOVEMBER 8, 2018
AROUND 11:05 A.M.

TROY'S SWEATY hands gripped the steering wheel so hard his knuckles hurt. The fire had jumped the road. Explosions and flames burst on both sides, chasing the Bronco from behind—a fire-breathing monster herding them toward the forest.

Mrs. Jones's warning came back to him . . . *You'll be heading straight into the forest. That's more dangerous than staying put.* He prayed she was wrong because there was no turning back.

The trees loomed ahead: more fuel to feed the raging blaze. Thick stands of it. He turned to look at his younger sister. Her eyes bulged in terror.

A wet rag still covered half of Emma's face to keep the smoke at bay, but it didn't stop her from screaming. Or flapping her arms and pointing everywhere at once. "The fire's all over the place. Look! There's another house in flames next to the road. And the bakery. It's in flames, too. You have to turn around. Go back the other way."

"We can't," he said, looking into the rearview mirror. It seemed as if the entire town behind them was lit with flames. "We have to keep going. It's our only chance."

"We're not going to make it," she said.

"Yes we are," he said, hoping the lie would morph into truth.

Rascal edged between the bucket seats again and tried to climb into the front.

"Back, girl," he ordered the dog. "Emma, please stop. You're wasting your breath. You'll only choke on more smoke. We'll be fine if we don't panic. Wet your face-rag again. And pour water on Rascal's head and on Midnight in the backpack. But don't let him out."

Emma's shrieks turned into sniffles as she did what she'd been told.

The cat yowled.

"Midnight doesn't like getting wet. He's not too happy. He scratched my hand."

"Don't worry. He'll forgive and forget."

"I'm sorry," Emma said. "I didn't mean to act like a baby." She rubbed the scratch on her hand. "Do you really think we're going to be okay?"

"Yeah," Troy said, even though he wasn't sure. Fire spots had sprouted on both sides of the highway. "We just have to get out of town. Which is what we're doing."

The car in front of them ground to a sudden halt and Troy almost rammed into its back bumper. What was the driver thinking? Why was he stopping when it was obvious the traffic in front of the guy was still moving? Why was he blocking up the whole lane? This was the only way out of town—unless you made a U-turn, and headed back into the fire.

Troy hit the horn—tapped a message urging the car to move. The pickup truck on Troy's bumper did the same.

It was like the stopped driver hadn't heard. The fire from behind bore down on them in an avalanche of molten ash. "Move," Troy ordered the parked car. "Can't you see? We're sitting ducks."

Heat from the fire pressed into the car through the rolled-up windows. Troy knew he couldn't wait a second longer. He wrenched the steering wheel right, pressed the gas, bumped up over the curb, and drove around the car. He tried to look inside, wondering why they'd stopped.

He couldn't see anything. Part of him felt like he should check on the driver. Part of him was afraid to waste precious time. If they'd wanted a ride, he reasoned, they would have jumped out and flagged him down.

A siren wailed. Flashing lights appeared in his rearview mirror and raced toward him. He let out a breath in relief. Finally, the firefighters had shown up. Or the police.

Emma twisted in her seat. "Boo. I thought it was a fire truck. It's an ambulance. And it's leaving town, too." It passed them on the left in the empty lane for oncoming traffic. "Hey, that's not fair."

"What's not fair?" Troy asked.

"They get to drive in that lane and no one else does."

"That's because the fire trucks will need to use it when they come racing into town to fight the fire."

"When are they coming?" Emma asked. "Shouldn't they have been here by now?"

He stared at her, his mind turning. "You know what? You're not so dumb after all. At least, not all the time."

He steered into the open lane and hit the gas. Freedom at last! Who cared if he was driving the wrong way down the oncoming lane? He sped along the open road, past the slug-train of law-abiding drivers. Other cars pulled out to chase after him as he zoomed to catch up with the ambulance's flashing lights.

The opening lyrics to *Ain't No Stoppin' Us Now* burst out of his mouth. A little muffled by the face-rag. Usually, he only sang in the shower, but he couldn't help himself. The town limits were just ahead. It felt like they were going to make it.

Emma let out a whoop and joined in. "We're on the move!"

CHAPTER 16

THEY WERE FLYING DOWN the road now, but inside the car, it felt like an oven cranked up to broil. Troy kept two car lengths between the Bronco and the ambulance in case it had to stop suddenly.

Both vehicles were doing forty miles per hour, and it was the fastest he'd ever driven.

"You should go on *America's Got Talent*," Emma said through the rag that covered her mouth. She bounced on the seat like a hot potato. "You could win. And get rich. And we could go somewhere cool. Like Africa. We could take Rascal and Midnight. They could meet their cousins. You could ride an elephant. I'd pet a lion."

"Africa's hot," he said. He swiped sweat from his forehead with the back of his hand. "The equator runs right through it. I'd rather be somewhere cold."

"Oh." Emma stopped bouncing. And although he couldn't see her mouth, he knew she'd lost the smile he'd heard in her voice. Instead, she stared out the windshield at a giant piece of ash gusting and swirling in the headlights. "Me, too."

Troy could have slapped his head except he was afraid to take his hands off the steering wheel. Why did he have to ruin Emma's daydream? She'd forgotten the danger they were in for a moment and he'd brought her back to reality.

"Let's pretend," he said. "It's snowing real snow out there. Like in, what's that movie?"

She shrugged.

"You know," he said, playing dumb. "The cartoon. The one with that weird-looking snowman with the funny name. Otis? Oopsie?"

"Olaf," Emma said, sitting straighter. "And he's not weird looking. He's cute. And he's funny. The movie's called—"

"Wait. Don't tell me. I got it," Troy said. His eyes were trained on the gap between the Bronco and the ambulance. "*Chilled*."

Emma rolled her eyes. "*Frozen*. It's called *Frozen*."

"Chilled. Frozen. Same thing." He forced a laugh. An annoyed Emma was preferable to a terrified Emma. "That's what I'd like right now. A gallon of frozen cookie-dough ice cream."

Emma said nothing.

"What would you like?" he asked her. "If you could have anything right now? This second."

A shower of flaming embers dropped from the sky, igniting trees and vegetation.

"For this to stop."

"Emma," Troy said. "Wet down Rascal and Midnight again. And splash more water on your face-rag. Save enough for mine."

She went to work, focusing on her task instead of what was going on outside. Flames engulfed the east side of the road, devouring trees like a starving dragon.

A shower ball of embers landed on the ambulance. It slowed and seemed to weave in the lane. Had the driver taken in too much smoke?

Troy tried to stay calm as he steered his vehicle through the smoke and flames. Everywhere, the patchy flares merged to become walls of fire moving closer to the road. He slowed and left more space between him and the ambulance.

A Honda Accord from the slower lane took advantage of the gap; it darted in front of the Bronco. Another car tried to do the same, but Troy sped up. The car clipped their rear bumper. The whole frame shuddered and the Bronco swerved. Troy fought the wheel for control. Maybe he should have let them in but he'd promised to keep Emma safe.

"No. No. No. No. No. No. No. No," Emma chanted in rhythm to a new sound of scraping, bumping metal that was now coming from the back of the vehicle.

"Emma?"

She kept up her mantra. The car behind began to blare its horn.

"Emma! Stop. Roll down the window. Use the flashlight and tell me what's making that noise."

Coughing, she craned her head out. "I can't see anything."

"Nothing's on the tire?"

"No."

"It must be the bumper dragging on the ground," Troy said. "Roll up the window. Ignore it."

In front of the Honda Accord, the ambulance slid to a stop and parked sideways in the lane. The Honda Accord swerved to miss it and landed in the left ditch. Troy stopped dead center in the lane. It was obvious no one was going anywhere for at least a minute or two.

He jumped out and raced to the back of the Bronco. The pavement was as hot as the surface of Mars at noon. As he'd suspected, the bumper was dragging. Another driver got out and joined Troy.

"Let me help you pull that off," the man said.

"It's fine," Troy said.

"No, it's not fine. It's creating sparks. We got to get it off."

"Should have thought of that."

Troy grabbed the loose end, and the man pulled the attached section. Together they wrenched the bumper free and tossed it to the side.

"Thanks," Troy managed, his skin feeling so tight and hot it felt like he'd been sunburned.

"Look out," the man shouted and raced back to his car.

Burning tree limbs were crashing to the ground. One smashed onto the road just five feet from where Troy stood. It shattered into a volley of sparks. The noise and blazing light rooted Troy to the spot.

A flying spark zapped his arm, stinging him into motion. He wrenched opened the Bronco's door just as a huge burning limb dropped onto the roof of the ambulance.

He stared opened-mouthed as the vehicle caught fire.

CHAPTER 17

EMMA STARTED TO SHRIEK. "It's on fire. It's on fire."

Troy dry-swallowed. If the flames reached the ambulance's gas tank, it would explode like a bomb. He slammed the gearshift into reverse and tried to back up. Except he couldn't—only a few feet separated the Bronco and the car behind them.

The car was hot. "Emma, grab three waters. Pass me one."

She handed it over.

"Thanks. Splash more water on your head and face. Take a drink and see to Midnight."

Troy used half the water to wet his hair, face-rag, and shoulders. It was warm but felt soothing. He poured the other half on Rascal's head and back. Tossing the empty, he opened the second bottle and took a long swig.

"Drink," he told Emma as he made a cup with his hand and poured water for Rascal. "Try to get Midnight to drink some, too."

Overhead, a roaring whoop-whoop-whoop beat the air.

"What's that noise?" Emma asked.

"I don't know."

From above, a bright beam spot-lit the gridlock of cars, tracing over them.

Emma leaned into the windshield, twisted and looked skyward. "It's a helicopter. I've never seen one so close."

The whoop-whoop-whoops grew louder.

"It's got a bucket hanging down. It's tipping, like a teapot. Oh!" She jerked back.

A gush of water doused the ambulance. Seconds later, water splashed onto the Bronco's roof and trickled down the windows.

The windshield made a cracking noise and a tiny one-inch line appeared on the driver's side at eye level.

Noooo . . . Don't let it grow any bigger.

Troy kept the thought inside. Maybe Emma wouldn't notice the crack. And if she did, she probably wouldn't realize what would happen if it ran the length of the window.

The windshield was more than just a windshield.

It was a fire-shield.

CHAPTER 18

THE AMBULANCE BACKED out of its skid, straightened and shot down the road. In less than twenty seconds it was headed down the highway once again. Lights flashing. Siren wailing.

Another wall of fire flared on the west flank. Trees glowed neon-orange about fifty yards to the right, half the length of a football field. It was moving fast, like ten yards every couple of minutes—an infernal quarterback going for the touchdown.

"Go! Go! Go!" Emma shouted like she was his personal cheerleader.

Troy gunned the engine and tried to close the gap between him and the flashing lights. Half of the other cars had the same idea at the same time. His only advantage was that he was already in the lane.

They flew down the highway toward safety. The ambulance led the charge like a beacon of life. Troy hardly noticed the side roads they passed as he drove. Concentrating on the road, he tried to ignore the spot fires igniting along on both sides of the pavement.

It looked like it was clearing up ahead.

Troy whooped. They were going to make it. They were out-running the fire.

Emma started to sing again. *"Ain't No Stoppin' Us Now!"*

He tapped the song's rhythm on the steering wheel and slowed for a sharp curve in the road. The ambulance had shot ahead, followed by the other lead cars except for one. A Corvette. Troy accelerated to close the gap between them when it happened.

A giant fir tree toppled, smashing onto the pavement. The song died on Emma' lips. The Corvette skidded and shot across the road in front of them and landed in the ditch. The downed tree had blocked their only escape.

Troy swerved and just missed clipping the Corvette before coming to a stop. He gulped in air. Unless miracles were real, they weren't going anywhere.

Emma squealed.

Rascal nosed his ear and licked.

"Don't panic, Emma," Troy said. "You okay?"

"Yes." Emma's voice was barely a whisper.

"Good."

He checked the rearview mirror. The fire behind had morphed into a unified giant wall of flames headed toward them—licking and consuming everything in its path.

A Dodge Ram Truck passed him on the right and rammed the downed tree. The truck high-centered on the tree trunk, but the tree didn't move. The driver jumped out, ran through the flames and disappeared from view.

Troy watched the truck's tires catch fire and burn. He wanted to cry but for Emma's sake, he kept up his brave front.

"What do we do now?" she asked.

"Let me think," he said, knowing they were going nowhere. He stared at the burning pickup and tree. Looked left at the Corvette in the ditch. Looked right and saw a dirt side-road winding into the trees. Checked the review mirror. Behind them, the two-lane road had turned into an eerie car lot. Cars were parked at odd angles. Headlights aimed uselessly at their doom.

What were the people in them thinking?

Up until that moment, even though Troy had been afraid, he'd believed they'd make it out. For the first time since he'd received Jeremy's text, real fear crept into Troy's gut. He felt numb. His mouth had gone dry. His heart ached.

He'd failed.

Failed to convince Mrs. Jones to leave.

Failed his parents.

Failed to protect his sister.

Failed to protect their pets.

They were going to die.

He swallowed hard, turned off the ignition and shut off the headlights.

CHAPTER 19

TROY!" Emma said. "What's that?"

She pointed to a pair of bright lights to her right. They were high in the air, like the headlights on a big semi-truck. But what would a semi-truck be doing on a small dirt road in the middle of the forest? And why were trees being knocked down in its wake?

He squinted, flipped on the headlights, and started the Bronco. Whatever it was, he wanted to be seen.

The big vehicle half-straddled the ditch and the shoulder as it drove. It was huge—a yellow Bulldozer with a wide blade raised in front like a shield.

"It's an earthmover. To cut roads," he said, grinning. "Like Scrapper."

"Who?"

"Scrapper," Troy repeated. He shifted into reverse and

looked back. "He's a *Constructicon.*"

"A what?" she asked.

"A kind of Transformer." He backed the SUV and stopped two feet from the Volkswagen Beetle parked behind them in the road. "He's one of the good guys."

"Oh," Emma said. "Is it going to save us?"

"I hope so."

The Bulldozer crept onto the road. Its running tracks tore into the pavement as it inched toward the pickup and the downed tree. At the same time, the giant blade lowered itself to the ground. In one big move, it shovel-scooped the pickup and burning tree off to the side of the road.

The driver looked back and waved for the cars to move.

Troy beeped a thank you and put the Bronco in drive. He rolled down his window and yelled to the man. "Do you need a ride? We have room."

The man shook his head. "I've got my ride. And work to do."

"You sure?"

"Yeah, a lot of people live off the grid. I'm clearing their side roads so they can get out. My partner is working the east fork. You go on now."

"Thanks!" Troy repeated.

"Thank you, Mr. Scrapper," Emma yelled in Troy's ear.

"Get going," the man said. "You're not out of the woods yet."

Troy gave him a salute and pressed the gas pedal.

"We're on the road again," Emma sang out and then laughed. "You hate that song, don't you?"

"Not at the moment," he said, thankful Emma couldn't read his mind. Or feel his fear.

God, if you're real. Let us outrun this fire.

CHAPTER 20

THEY WERE MOVING AGAIN. Troy drove at a steady clip. Not too fast. Not too slow. He was getting pretty good at this driving business. A few cars passed him when they hit the first straightaway but he didn't care. It looked like they were all going to outrun the fire.

"See, I told you we were going to make it," he said.

"Then why are those cars stopped?" Emma asked, pointing up ahead. "What's wrong now?"

"I don't know. Not again."

He took his foot off the gas and let the Bronco coast until they reached the cluster of cars before coming to a stop.

Troy saw a man climb out of his car and jog over to a parked Jeep.

"Stay here with Rascal and Midnight," Troy ordered.

"Where are you going?"

"To see what's up. I'll be fast." He got out of the Bronco. It was hot and super windy, like someone had turned on a blast furnace.

"I'm timing you," she said, her eyes bloodshot and scared above the bandana. She twisted in her seat and looked back. "And so is the fire."

Troy glanced back at the route they'd driven to get this far. The fire was advancing—moving fast. Ahead, the cars weren't moving at all. In the gloom, he could see a few people getting out of their cars and running down the road.

God, if you're real, this is the time to show yourself. Tell me what to do.

He didn't hear an answer.

Troy looked back at the approaching wall of flames. Watched it licking trees and tasting the sky. Knew it wasn't stopping its rampage. Where were the firefighters? Why weren't they coming? Didn't anyone care? A lot of people were going to die. And why didn't they send more than one helicopter? Didn't they know what was happening?

He made a split-second decision and ran to the passenger side of the car.

He yanked open the door. "Get out. We're going to run for it."

"What about Midnight and Rascal?"

"Rascal can run. Give me the backpack."

She handed it to him.

Troy held the backpack to his chest and slipped the straps over his shoulders. He remembered the flashlight and grabbed it. They wouldn't use it until they had to.

"You've got it on backward," Emma said.

"I know." He crouched with his back to her. "Climb on. I can run faster with you riding piggyback than I can dragging you."

She giggled nervously and climbed on.

"Hold tight," Troy said and set off at a fast jog. His face-rag slapped his mouth. "Come on Rascal. Good girl."

He knew all-out sprinting would be a mistake, unless absolutely necessary. It'd tire him too soon and he'd inhale too much smoke deep into his lungs. Rascal kept pace at an easy dog-trot. Midnight bounced on his chest and yowled a complaint.

Troy and Emma both began to hack and cough. He wouldn't stop until they were safe. Or . . . the fire caught them.

He ran past parked cars—some with people still sitting in them. Others abandoned like the Bronco. He and Emma weren't the only ones running for their lives.

He stumbled but managed to stay on his feet. His chest and legs hurt, but that wouldn't stop him.

Behind them, pops of shattering glass went off like fire-crackers. He chanced a backward glance and saw cars burning. It was time to sprint.

"Don't look back," he told Emma, hoping she hadn't seen anything. He didn't want to think about the people still in their cars. And he didn't want Emma to, either.

Rascal raced ahead.

"Wait, girl!" he yelled. "Stay with us."

Rascal ignored his command and ran toward the side of the road about twenty feet away.

Then Troy spotted the fox.

Rascal chased it over the bank and into the woods.

"Rascal! Come back."

Troy ran toward where the dog had disappeared, calling her name.

"Why did Rascal run away?" Emma asked.

They'd reached the spot and Troy stopped. He gasped for breath. "You're going to have to run for a bit. Okay?"

She nodded.

"Rascal," he yelled again. Emma joined him.

He looked back at the fire. They had to keep going.

CHAPTER 21

TEARS STREAKED from Emma's eyes into her face-rag. She voiced the words he'd been thinking. "Why did Rascal run away from us?"

"I don't know," Troy said, panting. Each breath felt like it was wrenched from his lungs. He'd had Rascal longer than he'd had a little sister. "But we have to keep going. Come on, climb back on."

"But you said—"

"Forget what I said. Get on my back." He turned and bent his knees. "Up you go."

Barking came from the woods. Rascal burst through the smoke. Emma flung her hands around the dog. "She didn't leave us. Did you, girl?"

Rascal barked again, nipped Troy's hand and grabbed

the cuff of his hoodie—pulled hard, tried to drag him down the steep embankment and away from the road.

"NO!" Troy said, pulling his hand free. "We've got to go this way."

The dog let go and ran down the hill a few paces, stopped, turned back, barked again. She waited. Tail wagging. When Troy didn't follow, she raced back up the bank. She grabbed him again and pulled hard enough to make him lose his footing.

Suddenly he was sliding down the steep bank of loose rocky soil. He felt his jeans rip and the flashlight jab into his ribs. Midnight yowled and thrashed in the backpack as he slid to a stop at the bottom. Rascal yelped and licked his face.

Emma scrambled down after them. Rascal barked once more and pushed through a wall of brush.

"Rascal," Emma cried as she helped Troy to his feet. "She wants us to follow her."

He looked up. They'd never be able to climb back to the road and outrun the fire now. It was better to keep going down.

Maybe Emma was right. Rascal wanted them to follow her into the wilderness. And then he remembered a Boy Scout camping trip he'd gone on two years earlier. They'd spent a weekend roughing it somewhere near here. It wasn't a real campground, but it had a stream running through it.

He jumped up, grabbed Emma's hand and pulled her into the brush, going as fast as they could manage. He had a stupid thought. *Don't let it be poison oak. That's all they'd need if they survived.*

Rascal kept up her frantic barking, leading them down into a narrow ravine.

Troy's legs were cramping. He didn't think he could walk much further, let alone run. And he knew Emma couldn't either.

"Where is Rascal taking us?" Emma asked.

They stepped from the thicket and found themselves at the edge of a shallow stream. Rascal was gulping water.

"Good girl. You led us to water," Troy said.

Emma waded in, but the water only came to her ankles. "It feels good. Hurry. Get in."

Troy stepped into the creek. The water was icy cold. It did feel good, but it wasn't deep enough to save them from a raging fire. They needed to find a hole at least three feet deep and big enough for all of them.

"We have to keep moving," Troy said. "Look at the hill." Flames were spilling down it. Trees and brush flared as the fire claimed them. "Stay in the center of the stream. Hold onto the back of my shirt to keep your balance. Okay?"

"Okay."

He pulled out the flashlight and switched it on, pointing it into the water to keep an eye out for boulders. They couldn't afford to trip now. The four of them sloshed down the center of the shallow creek. It widened for about forty feet before it narrowed again.

Troy smiled. *Maybe there was a God* because the water was growing deeper with each step. When it reached his knees, he raised the light.

He knew where they were, recognized the big rock at the edge of the swimming hole that his Boy Scout troop had splashed in for a whole week. Another thirty feet and they'd be there.

On the hill, the fire was picking up speed. Hot wind whipped the air. Embers swirled like fireflies, lighting mini-flares in their wake.

"Hurry," he said. "Almost there."

He started to run, slipped on submerged rocks—wind-milled his arms and fought to keep balance. Emma slid but held on, dragging his shirt down until it almost choked him.

He managed to dig his feet in and grabbed her arm. They stood panting for a moment.

He pointed at the flames. "We don't have much time."

Troy picked Emma up, squishing the backpack in the process. Midnight cried.

"You're hurting him," Emma sobbed and struggled to get free.

"He'll be fine," Troy said and slogged ahead with Emma in his arms.

She stopped fighting and Troy struggled to make the last few feet without dropping her.

Rascal splashed on ahead.

Five feet. Four Feet. Three. Two. One. They made it to the rock. Hopefully, the little swimming hole was as big as Troy remembered.

CHAPTER 22

TROY SET EMMA next to the rock.

The fire was raging down the hill. They didn't have much time.

The creek water was barely above his knees. He swept the flashlight's beam left and right. The hole was much smaller than he remembered. He'd have to make it work. He prayed it was big enough for the four of them.

"Hold on to the rock," he told her. "And make your way around to the other side. I'm going to check it out. I think it's deeper."

The water came up to his waist, but the hole was small —only half the size of a hot tub. It would do. It would have to. He slipped off the backpack with Midnight growling inside and carefully set it on the rock. The bag wobbled and rolled as Midnight fought to get free.

Troy had more important things to worry about. Like getting his sister into the pool before the fire attacked the trees and brush alongside the stream.

"What's taking you so long?" he said, and he slipped back around the rock.

"My foot's stuck," Emma said. "Between two rocks."

He heard a splash. Hoped it wasn't Midnight. He rushed to Emma and pulled on her leg.

"That hurts."

"I'm sorry. But the fire will be here any second."

A large flaming leaf floated down and hit the water with a hiss.

Troy reached into the cool water and felt for her foot. Her shoe was wedged between the large rock and a smaller boulder. He wished he could see what he was doing. Wished he didn't have to hurt her but knew he had to get her foot free.

Using both hands he felt the shoe again. It was her favorite hot pink high-top Converse. He fumbled with the laces. Why did his sister always have to tie a double knot?

The fire had reached the bottom of the ravine. A thicket of brush, like the one they'd pushed through, burst into flames.

Frantically he pulled at the laces, loosening them. Putting both hands around her ankle, he jerked.

She yelped but her foot slipped free. "What about my shoe?" she wailed.

"You can get it later."

He lifted her, took two steps and plopped her into the

deeper pool. Rascal was there, with the backpack in her mouth and Midnight crying from inside.

The flames lit the ravine. It looked like a movie filmed in Hades.

Emma screamed. "It's cold."

"Good girl, Rascal," he said and took the backpack. He unzipped it a quarter of an inch and let about two inches of water inside. Midnight howled in protest. There was a rock ledge. Troy set the backpack where Midnight wouldn't drown, half in and half out of the pool.

"Stay as low as you can," he said. "Do what I do."

He dunked his head. The cool closed around his steaming scalp. It felt awesome. After a long second, he raised his nose and mouth just high enough to breathe. Next, he pulled the rag from his face, soaked it and put it on his head like a hat. Rascal huddled, propped on Troy's lap. Emma clung to them both.

They stared at each other as the fire overtook the little canyon. Other than dunking Midnight's bag and re-soaking their rag hats, they waited in silence, hoping the fire would burn itself out.

It took ten minutes for the water to go from ice-cold to cool. After ten more minutes, the water barely felt luke-warm. It took another ten minutes for the stream to turn hot. Really hot. Then, the shallow river became the hottest hot tub Troy had ever soaked in.

For what seemed like an hour, it felt like they were boiling and being cooked alive. His heart was slamming. His hands and feet began to swell. He wanted to get out, but knew they couldn't.

The fire raged so loud, it sounded like an endless freight train headed for the underworld. The crackling roar seemed to go on forever and ever.

CHAPTER 23

BUTTE COUNTY, CALIFORNIA
THURSDAY, NOVEMBER 8, 2018
AROUND 12:37 P.M.

TROY EASED his ears out of the water. The silence felt deafening. Not a single bird chirped. No sounds of movement came from the forest. At first, it seemed darker without the flames.

A sweet wind whipped over him, bringing smoke and then taking it away.

"Come on." Troy straightened, rising until his shoulders were clear of the water. The air was still smoky but not as bad as before. He motioned for Emma to rise, pulled the rag from his head, dipped it, and washed his face. "It's cooler now out of the water."

Emma bobbed up next to him. Her face looked puffy. She was crying.

"We're going to be okay," Troy said and helped her

stand. "The fire is gone and I think the sky is starting to turn gray. Out you go, Rascal."

With more room in the pool, he stood. Hot water streamed off him. He breathed in. It still smelled like he was in the wrong seat at a campfire. But after being submerged for at least forty-five minutes in near-scalding water, the air felt amazingly cool.

The hungry monster fire had run away in search of more fuel to devour. Smoke hung in the air. Here and there, it rose from the scorched earth in wisps.

He squinted in the dim light, but it was still too dark to really see well. The few trees he could just make out looked like scorched skeletons. The bushes had been reduced to heaps of ashes.

"I'm hot," Emma said. She peeked into the backpack. "And so is Midnight. Shhh. You're okay. As soon as we get somewhere safe you can get out."

"Don't worry, we'll cool down now," he said.

He thought of their last mad dash down the hillside, of the fox and of Rascal pulling at his sleeve. How lucky they'd been to find this pool of water! As he stared at his sister, he started to grin.

"What are you smiling for?" she demanded.

"We made it. We did it! We made it out."

She started to smile, too. "You're right. We did, didn't we? We made it!"

"Yep. Maybe there is a God."

She wiped her eyes, water dripping from her hair. "Of course, you silly," Emma said, "I learned all about him in Sunday school."

He rolled his eyes.

Rascal barked and scrambled onto the creek bank.

"Now that the fire's over," Emma said. "I need my shoe."

Troy laughed and gave his sister a knuckle rub to the head.

"Hey," she said and punched his shoulder. "I'm telling Mom."

CHAPTER 24

BUTTE COUNTY, CALIFORNIA
THURSDAY, NOVEMBER 8, 2018
AROUND 1:12 P.M.

THEY FOLLOWED the creek back to where Troy thought they'd come down the embankment. He couldn't be sure. The world was colored in shades of gray. It felt like they'd stepped into a black-and-white movie. The only color came from orange embers still glowing here and there, clinging to life.

Nothing in the forest was left untouched.

In the eerie silence, they crept along, careful to keep their feet away from the burning coals. Emma carried Midnight, but kept the cat in the bag. If he ran away, she'd never find him.

Rascal kept pace at Troy's side.

"You're a good girl," he said, patting her head. "You saved us."

Up ahead, he spotted the fire-scarred hillside. He felt pretty sure it led up to the road. They stopped at the bottom for a short rest.

"Can I call Mom and Dad?" Emma said.

"Why not?" Troy said, tearing the rag he'd used as a facemask into strips.

She frowned. "Can I use your cell? Mine got wet."

He grinned and pulled his cell from his back pocket. "Mine, too." He laughed. "Not sure we have service here, anyway."

Emma eyed the rag strips. "What are you going to do with those?"

Troy pointed to the smoking ground. "Rascal doesn't have shoes. The ground's hot."

"Oh," Emma said. "I see. You're going to make her shoes." She frowned. "Do you think it'll work?"

"If it doesn't, I'll carry her. Rascal. Come here, girl." Troy sat on the ground and carefully wrapped the rag strips around all four of his dog's feet and tied them. When he was done, Rascal sniffed them and then bounded up the hill, barking as she raced to the top.

Troy and Emma followed.

He wondered what they'd find at the top. When he came over the lip of the hill, he glanced left and right.

The strip of asphalt snaked away into the gloom. Not a single car was in sight.

Rascal lay on the road panting and trying to chew the makeshift shoes from her feet. Troy squatted next to the dog and unwound the rags. He wrapped them into a ball and shoved them into the front belly pocket of his hoodie.

"Why are you keeping those?"

Troy stood. "Just in case Rascal needs them again."

Emma's eyes went wide. "You don't think the fire's coming back?"

He shook his head. "There's nothing left to burn. Okay, ready for a hike?" he asked, stretching his back. He was still wary but was pretty sure they were safe.

He felt sore all over like someone had stuffed him in a sack and beat him with a baseball bat. But still, it felt good to be alive. Hiking was the last thing his feet wanted to do but they couldn't just sit there. "Let's hit the road."

"Why are we going this way instead of back home?" she asked. "Wouldn't Paradise be closer?"

"Probably, but Mom and Dad are this way. Remember? We said we'd head for Chico?" What he didn't tell her was that first of all, home was gone. Second of all, he didn't want to walk back past the cars that had burned. Third, the fire could still be burning back there and he'd had enough fire for a lifetime.

"You're limping," Emma said. "And you tore your jeans. And your face is dirty."

He grinned. "You think I look bad? Just be glad you don't have a mirror."

She slugged him in the shoulder.

"Hey! Take it easy."

She laughed.

Fifteen minutes later they heard engines coming up the road from the Sacramento Valley. Three minutes later, a caravan crawled around the corner—a caterpillar of red trucks and blinking lights. A horn blasted.

"Yeah!" Emma shouted and waved both arms. "Fire-fighters!"

"And a ride," Troy said, feeling the weight of responsibility being lifted from his shoulders.

The truth was, he was exhausted. Although they'd escaped the fire, he'd been afraid he didn't have the energy to get his sister back to civilization before he dropped.

The first truck didn't stop. The driver waved and shouted words that were lost in the engine's roar.

Three more vehicles drove past. Then another. And another.

Were they still on their own?

Wasn't anyone going to help them?

CHAPTER 25

A BIG RED pickup truck peeled away from the train of fire fighting vehicles and parked. A guy in fire protection gear hopped out.

"Hey, kids. Need a lift?"

"You could say that," Troy said.

"Even though we're not supposed to take rides from strangers," Emma said.

The man held out his hand. "Hi. I'm Tom Williams, Transportation. And from the looks of you, you must have had quite a morning. I can see you're a resilient pair of kids."

"Yes, we are," Emma said. "We were never going to give up. Right, Troy?"

"No, we didn't." Even though it had seemed hopeless at least a dozen times.

"What are your names?" Mr. Williams asked.

"Emma. Emma Benson." She took his hand and shook it. "This is my big brother Troy. Who's pretty cool sometimes when he's not being a boring pain. And that's Rascal." She lowered her voice. "Midnight's in the bag. So. Now we're not strangers, my feet would love a ride."

Mr. Williams laughed. "Climb in. You kids are incredible. Great job for making it through."

They piled into the front seat. Emma turned into *Chatty Cathy* and by the time they left the forest and reached the rolling fields of yellowed grass in the valley, she'd told the fireman their entire life history. Including both their mom's and dad's cell numbers.

"I had to memorize their numbers because I kept losing my phone," she said.

"You're a bright one," Mr. Williams said and handed her his phone. She passed it to Troy.

Emma rattled off a number and Troy punched it in. It didn't even make it through half a ring.

"Hello?" his dad said, sounding panicked.

"Dad. It's me. We're okay."

"Troy! Thank God? Where are you? You still driving? Emma's fine?"

"I want to talk," Emma said and grabbed the phone. "Me and Rascal, Midnight and Troy are just fine. A fireman is giving us a ride to—where are you taking us?"

"To an evacuation center in Chico." He gave her the address.

She repeated the information into the phone.

Troy took the phone back. "See you soon, Dad."

"Troy," his dad said. "I'm sorry we weren't there. I'm proud of you. We'll be waiting when you arrive.

The evacuation center was like a giant ant-farm of activity. People were everywhere. Coming. Going. Waiting. Arriving. Talking. Reporting.

An ambulance with flashing lights pulled out of the lot as they drove in.

Troy couldn't spot his parents in the chaos. Had they been held up on the road?

His eyes scanned everything at once. A stream of people carried cases of bottled water into the building. The Salvation Army had brought boxes and trays of food. The Red Cross had set up a medical triage station.

Mr. Williams parked the truck in a space reserved for CAL FIRE. A news-crew spotted them and pointed a camera their way. The reporter started toward them.

Emma pulled down the visor and looked in the mirror at her soot-streaked face, red eyes and crazy hair. "I don't want my picture taken," Emma said. "I just want to see Mom and Dad. Where are they? They said they'd be here."

"I'm looking," Troy said and spotted them. "There they are! See, Mom's waving."

"And running," Emma squealed. "Hurry up. Open the door, Troy."

Troy already had the door open. He turned to Mr. Williams. "Thanks for the ride."

"Good luck, kids," he said.

"Hurry, Troy." Emma pushed her brother's shoulder. He hopped out, followed by Rascal and Emma with Midnight.

"You did well," Mr. Williams said through the open

window of the truck. "Tell your dad he should be proud of you both." He shifted into reverse, waved and drove away.

"He didn't wait to meet Mom and Dad," Emma said.

"He doesn't have time," Troy said. "The fire isn't out."

Before Emma could say anything else, his parents reached them.

His mom was crying and scooped them all up, including Rascal, into a group hug.

"I've been so afraid," Mom said, squeezing them tight. She whispered in Troy's ear, "I love you. Thanks for keeping your sister safe."

Midnight yowled, not liking the squishing hug.

Mom released them and wiped tears from her cheeks. "You two need a bath. And clean clothes. We're going to Grandma's house."

"Can we stop for ice cream on the way?" Emma said. "We missed breakfast. I'm starving."

"Of course," Mom said.

"Dad?" Troy said. "Can I borrow your phone to send a text to Jeremy? I want to let him know I'm okay."

"Sure, son," Dad said and ruffled Troy's hair. "So proud of you."

"Really?"

"More than really. You kept your head. Saved your sister. Did the Benson name fine."

CHAPTER 26

```
TWO WEEKS LATER...
CHICO, CALIFORNIA
```

IT'S FUNNY, now that they couldn't go back to Paradise, he realized how much he missed the place. He missed being able to walk over to Jeremy's. He missed his old bedroom. He even missed the tire swing that had been busted on the front lawn. It would be a long time before life got back to normal. He was glad he had his family, though, and he knew that having survived the fire, they could get through anything together.

What was crazy, his dad had gotten a call that the Bronco had been located. It had been towed to a junkyard in Chico. If they couldn't go home, maybe some small memento had survived the fire.

"Do you think we'll find anything?" Troy asked as they pulled into the yard and parked.

"Maybe," Dad said. "Maybe not. We'll see."

Rows and rows of junked cars waited to be stripped of usable parts before being crushed. One whole row was made up of burnt vehicles from the fire.

They got out and Troy's dad went into the office. Troy started down the row of car skeletons.

The vehicles looked like they'd all been tricked-out by the same fire-breathing mechanic. Lights, bumpers, tires, chrome trims and any other pieces on the outside had melted. The paint jobs were scorched into angry patterns.

Troy found their Bronco near the end of the row. Its windows were gone and it looked like the others but seemed worse. Before the fire, it had been the coolest car ever. He put his hand on the rough metal and patted the hood like it was an old friend. "You got us through the worst of it," he said to the car.

Even though it had rained, the SUV still smelled of smoke and soot.

His dad and the yard-attendant joined him. "You're welcome to take what you find, but I doubt it'll be much," the man said.

Troy leaned in through the missing window. Everything from the seats to the ceiling had been charred. The only thing that appeared to have survived were the keys dangling from the ignition.

The man said, "You're lucky you kids didn't stay with the car."

Troy winced as he nodded, remembering his and Emma's final run.

The man returned to his office. Troy and his dad spent ten more minutes searching and came up empty-handed.

"Guess this was a wasted trip," Troy said.

"Don't know about that." Dad reached in through the

driver's door and pulled the key from the ignition. "I still have the keys to my first ride. You should have yours." He tossed them to Troy, who caught them easily.

Troy stared down at them and closed his fingers around them. He nodded. "Thanks."

"You know son, you're amazing. Your quick thinking saved you and your sister."

Troy smiled. Those keys were proof that the four of them had beaten the fire. He'd keep them forever as a trophy. They'd won. He'd driven the Bronco through flames. Kept his sister safe. Saved the family pets. Out-ran the fire on foot. Huddled in a stream while the fire raged through the ravine. But the Camp Fire didn't get them.

Troy felt like shouting, *I made it.*

I escaped California's deadliest fire!

The California Camp Fire raged on for 18 days.

Three people are still listed as missing.

Eighty-six people are listed as deceased.

More than 50,000 people were evacuated. Many are still struggling to find new homes.

Our thoughts are with the brave people and their pets whose lives were turned upside-down on that fateful day.

TEN FACTS ABOUT THE CALIFORNIA CAMP FIRE

- The Camp Fire is California's deadliest and most destructive wildfire.
- 6th deadliest wildfire in the US
- Many evacuees spent over 3 hours driving through the raging fire
- The blaze was so hot it melted cars and wheels, and reduced bodies to bone.
- It spread at 80 football fields a minute.
- 240 square miles burned. That's larger than the city of Chicago.
- The fire burned for 18 days: from November 8, 2018 at 6:29 a.m. until November 25, 2018
- The Camp Fire is named after where it began: near the Camp Creek and Pulga Roads, close to the Jarbo Gap in Butte County, CA. Fires are often named according to their starting location.
- Number of buildings destroyed: 13,972 homes, 528 restaurants, stores, offices, schools, churches, rest homes, and a hospital, plus 4,293 other structures.
- 50,000 people were evacuated and 86 people lost their lives.

CAMP FIRE TIMELINE
Thursday, Nov 8, 2018

- **6:30 a.m.** (approx.) Fire sparks to life near the Feather River.
- **6:51 a.m.** The fire now covers 10 acres.
- **7:23 a.m.** (one hour has passed) The first evacuation order for Pulga, CA is tweeted by the Butte County sheriff. Unfortunately, most residents do not receive the tweet.
- Wind speeds are approaching 50 miles per hour. The fire is growing rapidly. It's consuming the equivalent of a football field *every second*. (Cal Fire)
- The fire's speed makes it impossible for most Paradise residents to evacuate before it arrives.
- **Around 8 a.m.** The fire reaches the town of Paradise, CA.
- **10:30 a.m. It looks like night.**
- **10:45 a.m.** The fire has grown to nearly 20,000 acres. (satellite image records)
- **6 p.m.** Less than twelve hours have passed. The Camp Fire has traveled 17 miles and burned almost everything in its path.

DID YOU KNOW?

WHERE IS PARADISE, CALIFORNIA?

Longitude: 121.434700 Latitude: 39.813400

Paradise is located around one hundred and forty miles northeast of San Francisco and eighty miles north of California's state capital, Sacramento. The closest big town is Chico, around a forty-minute drive away. Until the fire, the small town was nestled in evergreen forests with beautiful views of the Sierra foothills.

WHO LIVED IN PARADISE?

Around 27,000 people lived in Paradise itself. According to the latest census, over twenty-five percent of its residents were 65-years or older. It has been described as a tight close-knit community.

WHAT WAS LOST?

Ninety percent of homes and buildings in Paradise were destroyed in the first twenty-four hours.

By November 11th, three days after the fire began, 52,000 people had been evacuated from Paradise and the surrounding area.

The *Honey Run Covered Bridge* nearby Butte Creek was the last three-span Pratt-style truss bridge in the United States. The fire incinerated it on November 10.

FAST FACTS
Start Date: 11/8/2018
Start Time: 6:29 a.m.
Incident Type: Vegetation Fire
Location: Camp Creek and Pulga Roads, Butte County
CAL Fire Unit: Butte County

WHAT CAUSED THE FIRE?

Power lines belonging to Pacific Gas and Electric caused the deadly fire.

The California Department of Forestry and Fire Protection said, *"After a very meticulous and thorough investigation, Cal Fire has determined that the Camp Fire was caused by electrical transmission lines owned and operated by Pacific Gas and Electricity located in the Pulga area."*

"The tinder dry vegetation and Red Flag conditions consisting of strong winds, low humidity and warm temperatures promoted this fire and caused extreme rates of spread."

Cal Fire said that a second ignition site was caused by *"vegetation into electrical distribution lines owned and oper-*

ated by PG&E." The second fire merged into the original fire, officials said.

A number of factors contributed to the spread of the blaze.

NO RAIN = LOW HUMIDITY

Although the five-year California drought had officially ended the previous April, Butte County had had no rain for seven months. While summers are normally hot and dry, autumn rains usually arrive long before November. This year they did not.

The state's water restrictions were still in effect. Yards were dry and kindle-ready.

HIGH WINDS + FIRE = DEVASTATION

Through the morning of November 9, the National Weather Service issued a *Red Flag high-wind warning* for most of Northern California's interior.

The high-wind warnings proved true.

Once the PG&E downed power lines touched the dry plants and sparked the fire, the wind took hold. A high-powered, fifty-mile-an-hour gale tore though the area, fanning the blaze and driving it forward.

The fire moved at a rate of eighty football fields per minute. No runner, no matter how fast, could cross eighty football fields in a minute. It took less than twenty-four hours for the flames to devour Paradise and its surrounding communities.

"Pretty much the community of Paradise is destroyed, it's that kind of devastation. The wind that was predicted came and just wiped it out," Captain Scott McLean (Cal Fire) said.

WHY WEREN'T PEOPLE WARNED IN TIME TO ESCAPE?

There are many reasons why people didn't receive the information to evacuate in time.

Living in the Sierra Foothills above the Sacramento Valley has a strong pull for those in search of small communities, a lower cost of living, less urban bustle or planning, beautiful views and less bureaucracy. With the warm summers, it's a great place to retire. It's a peaceful life, but it comes with a price.

Many homes don't have cell phone service, access to WiFi, or cable television. While this might seem strange to some, many retirees lived in Paradise, people who aren't tied to their devices. Unfortunately, this meant they did not have easy access to information, such as Tweets and emergency cell phone alerts.

Those with service in town were also at a disadvantage. One cell tower was down. Many homes had replaced their landlines for cell phones. Electricity was out, so TV was unavailable.

Butte County had actually beefed up its emergency warning notification system because of the 2017 California wildfires. However, their efforts were in vain. They sent evacuation warnings over landlines, cell phones, and Twitter. Unfortunately, only twelve percent of county residents had opted in to receive the reverse 911 notifications. The rest either failed to sign up or chose to opt out.

The fire moved too fast for officials to use other means of notifying residents, such as door-to-door warnings.

Most people found out about the evacuation by word-of-mouth from friends, neighbors, and/or family.

Some people chose to ignore the evacuation order until it was too late to escape.

BE INFORMED ABOUT WILDFIRES

- Sign up for emergency alerts.
- Know your community's evacuation plans and find several ways to leave the area. Drive the evacuation routes and find shelter locations. Have a plan for pets and livestock.
- Leave if told to do so.
- If trapped, call 9-1-1. Turn on lights to help rescuers find you.
- Listen for emergency information and alerts.
- Use N95 masks to keep particles out of the air you breathe.
- If you are not ordered to evacuate but smoky conditions exist, stay inside in a safe location or go to a community building where smoke levels are lower.

For more information, visit:
https://www.ready.gov/wildfires

THE I ESCAPED SERIES
I Escaped North Korea!

I Escaped The California Camp Fire

coming soon

I Escaped The World's Deadliest Shark Attack

Join the *I Escaped Club* to hear about new releases at:

https://tinyurl.com/escaped-club

ALSO BY SD BROWN
Code Orange Cancun

Escape To Molokai

Saving Bigfoot Valley

ALSO BY SCOTT PETERS
Mystery of the Egyptian Scroll

Mystery of the Egyptian Amulet

Mystery of the Egyptian Mummy

FANTASTIC BOOKS ABOUT FIRES

The Great Fire
by Jim Murphy

Uprising
by Margaret Peterson Haddix

What Was the Great Chicago Fire?
by Janet B. Pascal

Scout: Firefighter
by Jennifer Li Shotz

I Survived the Great Chicago Fire, 1871
Lauren Tarshis

RED CROSS RESOURCE

Print and discuss this PDF to help kids cope with disasters:
http://bit.ly/kidsfirePDF

I ESCAPED THE CALIFORNIA CAMP FIRE
STUDY GUIDE
https://tinyurl.com/escaped-fire